퇴역 레슬러

UEA PUBLISHING PROJECT
NORWICH

JEON SUNGTAE

OLD WRESTLER

Old Wrestler
Jeon Sungtae

Translated from the Korean by
Sora Kim-Russell

First published by
Strangers Press, Norwich, 2019
part of UEA Publishing Project

Distributed by
NBN International
10 Thornbury Road
Plymouth PL6 7PP
t. +44 (0)1752 202301
e.cservs@nbninternational.com

Printed by
Swallowtail, Norwich

Series editors
Nathan Hamilton & Deborah Smith

Editorial assistance
Senica Maltese

Cover design and typesetting
Glen Robinson

Illustration and Design Copyright © Glen Robinson, 2019

ISBN: 978-1-911343-59-2

This book is published with the support of the Literature
Translation Institute of Korea

Yeoyu ——
new voices
Korea

TRANSLATED BY SORA KIM-RUSSELL

It got so bad, he was like this...' The wrestler pressed his nose into the folded blanket on the edge of the bed and sniffed. 'Shoving his nose into his own shit just to smell something. That's how badly he missed it.'

The homecare nurse frowned, then started giggling. She laughed harder than the joke warranted.

'Sorry, it's not him I'm laughing at,' she said. 'It's you...'

'What?'

'You look like a puppy!'

'As a matter of fact, that's how he got the nickname Mutt. I swear! Everyone started calling him that afterward.'

The wrestler was excited for a moment. But despite how clear the image of his friend's face was, his memory of the event kept flickering in and out. He couldn't remember exactly when it had happened. He thought back over what he'd told the nurse. Why had he brought up that story in the first place? That's right — he'd been trying to tell her he was upset with her.

The story concerned a Japanese friend from his old gym who'd shattered his ankle in a car accident. The bone was set, a cast put on, and the ankle had healed, but to everyone's surprise, he'd complained that he couldn't smell anything anymore. A nerve connected to his olfactory senses had been damaged somehow. He became unable to detect certain aromas, while others were completely different to how he remembered them — the scent of flowers and the cosmetics worn by the nurses disgusted him most of all. It nearly drove him crazy. He would stick his nose into his food and weep. It got so bad that he shit on a piece of newspaper just to test whether he could smell it.

'You're in much better shape than he was, sir,' the nurse said. Her giggles had finally subsided. 'You recognised the smell of perilla oil in the sauteed onions this morning.'

The mention of onions reminded him why he was angry with her, on top of which he was frustrated at his inability to keep track of the conversation. But he decided to drop it. He wasn't in the mood to talk about it now, and anyway the moment had passed.

The nurse took his navy suit out of the closet.

'Sir, you remember the wedding today?'

As she tapped the front of the suit absentmindedly, fine dust billowed up in the sunlight that streamed through the window. He waved her off, unable to quell his annoyance fully.

'Where is it?'

'The Agricultural Co-op Hall. The photographer is coming to escort you.'

He thought about the hassle of visiting his home town. Why should he have to attend the wedding of some kid whose face he'd never even seen? But to the people of his home town he was a hero, a living legend. Back in his prime, he had built them a bridge to the mainland. Not with his own hands, of course. While placing the championship belt around his waist, the General had asked him what he wished for. Standing stiff and straight, the champion wrestler had recited the answer he'd rehearsed: His home town needed a bridge.

'Anything for someone like you, working so hard to help us build a new nation,' the General had said.

'Thank you, sir!'

Anyone in his place would have given the same answer. Back then, all sports heroes spoke of wanting paved roads, electricity, bridges. Whether or not they got them, everyone was moved by their requests, which ensured they returned home in full glory. The residents of their impoverished home towns would pool their money and work together to turn the hero's birthplace into a memorial hall, complete with a commemorative plaque out front. And the villagers wouldn't stop there. Any event, great or small, meant the heroes found themselves invited back as guests of honour. Their stories and legends got passed down through the generations and they were the pride of their home town for a very long time. It was an honour for which the wrestler was always thankful, but at the same time, it was a lot to ask of a hero who was now old and ailing.

The nurse left to look for a clothes brush. The wrestler walked over to the window, pushed a chair into the sunlight and sank slowly onto it as if dipping into a warm bath. Low rolling hills of onion fields reached halfway up into the mountains. With harvest underway, the fields in the foothills had already been shorn of onions and were baring their original reddish ochre soil in striking contrast to the lush green of the unharvested village fields below. The work was proceeding rapidly. There had to be at least fifty women labouring, most of them farmhands who'd made the journey over from the mainland. In a few days, the view of autumn fields outside this window would turn bleak and empty. Sunlight settled on the wrestler's cold knees.

He watched the women finish their work and walk together to the next field. Though it looked from that distance like a still life, he imagined he could hear their murmuring and feel the dust their feet kicked up from the earth. In the five days he'd been on the island, the voices of women were always what woke him. Sometimes it was their laughter and sometimes it was their singing that skimmed the thin layer of sleep from his mind. In half a lifetime of roaming abroad, he'd spent ten of those years, now forgotten by the rest of the world, in a hospital in Fukuoka, Japan. It was a civilian hospital with a large garden where every morning he'd been awoken by the raucous twittering of birds. There was nothing worse than being stuck in a foreign land, with nowhere to go, and suffering terrible nightmares every night, but the birdsong had very gently and easily crumbled the boundary between the inside and outside of sleep. He imagined the women's voices as they harvested onions to sound like bird chatter, the same mix of effervescence and languor.

Since returning home, his mornings had been relaxing. His mood buoyed by waking every day to the fresh, green scent of onion plants, he'd excitedly asked his nurse several times if she smelled the onions too. She shook her head at first, but after he'd repeated the question a couple more times, she admitted that her chronic rhinitis made it difficult for her to smell anything. She stuck her entire head out the window and took a deep sniff of the air, but the look on her face said she couldn't smell a thing.

'The island always...' He'd felt suddenly choked up. 'It always smelled like onions around this time of year.'

With those words, the scent of onions had seemed to grow even stronger. It reminded him even more of why he had come back. He felt relieved to know that his senses were still functioning, despite the doctors' concerns, and that risking the discomfort of long-distance travel in order to come home had been the right choice after all.

He had been wracked with nightmares the whole time he was in the hospital. Nightmares in which he opened up his own skull and gazed down at his brain, which had turned as stiff as a stale rice cake. The image spilled over from his dreams and into his waking life. Each time he was reminded that he was losing to the illness, that scene from his dream conjured itself again and pursued him. The dream had grown more frequent with each passing day and even came to him in his brief interludes of dozing off. His doctor increased his aspirin dosage. But it only temporarily stilled the nightmares and daytime visions; less than a month would pass before they found him again. Then, one day, the nightmares and visions stopped suddenly, of their own accord. Instead of dissipating, his doubts grew. He'd had a vague premonition that his brain would eventually harden completely, leaving him incapable of either dreams or visions, and it seemed that day had come. So when the nightmares finally returned, he breathed an actual sigh of relief. The anxiety brought on by the dreams was better than no dreams at all.

After that, a new symptom had appeared. He summoned the nurse. She'd forgotten to give him his usual injection, which was unlike her.

'I need my shot,' he'd said, face down on the bed as always, pushing his pants down.

'Which shot are you talking about?' The nurse sounded surprised. She flipped through his chart. 'You just had one this morning. I gave it to you myself.'

These lapses happened over and over.

11

Eventually he had to go for more boring, painful exams. When the results came in, his doctor spoke carefully.

'Your condition has grown rather complicated. We need to observe you for a few more days, but based on the current results, it seems that toxins have begun building up in your brain. It's not just a problem with the blood vessels. Excess hormone secretion is wreaking havoc on your neurotransmitters. I'm going to put you on Aricept three times a week. As long as you don't skip any of your dosages, your condition shouldn't worsen. And I know I told you this before, but you've got to try to avoid any further stress.'

He understood the doctor's warning. There was no treatment that could reverse the damage done to his brain. All they could do was slow the inevitable. On top of the image of his old brain hardening, he saw another of the brain tissue turning black.

The scent of onions had returned his early childhood mornings to him. Awakening to that fresh, green scent amid the sharp smoke of the cooking fire. Hearing the clanging of a cowbell and opening the door to see a cow chewing on its feed, the breath from its nostrils steaming in the cool air. And from the kitchen, the warm, inviting sound of pot lids clattering. The memories were clearly gifts from his home town. As they resurfaced, so too did the hope that his slowly dying senses would recover. He wanted to rush out of the house at once and visit every last corner of the island, take in the scent of soil warmed by the spring sun, carve the names of his childhood friends into the bark of old trees. He wanted to run to the water's edge and watch the waves at work. He wanted to fill his lungs with their salt air.

But he'd been depressed again since the previous afternoon. After lunch, he had slipped into a nap for over an hour. The nurse must have used that time to slip away herself, into the onion

12

fields. She'd probably risked the brief outing to ease the boredom of having no one else to talk to. Considering that she usually spent her days cooped up in a hospital, the trip would've felt like a long-awaited vacation. She'd lived in the city for all of her fifty years, so the unfamiliar scenery of island life was bound to stir her curiosity. And besides, the April sunlight was too beautiful and dazzling to just sit and stare out a window.

She had reappeared in his room carrying a red mesh bag half full of onions and dumped them on a table. 'It's like all the onions in the world come from here. Nothing but onion plants, as far as the eye can see,' she'd grumbled. 'When I told them you were back, they gave me these free of charge. They told me to take as many as I wanted, but this is all I could carry.'

Her face had flushed as she kept chattering.

'That guy who calls himself Mun Ik-jeom is funny. He said you probably know him, too. He's been the village foreman for the last ten years or so. He compared himself to the original Mun Ik-jeom, except instead of bringing cotton seeds to Korea, he brought onion seeds to the island. He said he's the one who first planted onions here, back during the New Village Movement in the 1970s. He's so proud of himself for coming up with the idea of switching to them from barley.'

The moment he had heard those words, he'd felt like he'd been picked up and thrown out of the ring. If what his nurse said was true, then the village had only been growing onions for the last twenty years – that is, after he'd left home. Did that mean that the scent he'd narrowly managed to dredge from his damaged brain was not the scent of onions, but of barley? And who'd ever heard of the scent of barley anyway? He may as well have been smelling nothing at all. It had filled him with dismay. All at once, he'd remembered his doctor warning him that it was

13

possible to fool your own senses, to smell things that weren't really there, just by picturing them vividly.

His dismay had turned to anger. The nurse clearly hadn't listened to a word he'd said. If only she were a little more attentive, she'd have known better than to so carelessly share what she'd heard in the fields. In fact, he couldn't help but feel betrayed by how excited she was now compared to her reaction when he'd first told her he was planning a trip home.

'Sir, the photographer is here.'

He jumped at the sound of the nurse's voice; she hadn't even bothered to knock but had instead aimed the words at the back of his head. By the time he turned around, she had already vanished through the half-open door.

The photographer was getting shots of the framed photos hanging in the living room, panning from left to right without moving his eye from the viewfinder. The wrestler stood back so as not to get in his way. The photos were in no particular order. It looked like the nurse had simply hung the largest photos first. There was one of him in his twenties, holding onto the reins of a cow that he'd just won in a match (seeing it a few days ago had reminded him that he used to wear white shoes), and another of him in his forties, wearing a fedora, flanked by two blond actresses. (They were Hollywood actresses, but he couldn't remember their names.)

The photographer pointed the lens at a photo of him, hands raised like claws, facing off against a white opponent. It was Lou Thesz, an American wrestler and heavyweight champion. He couldn't remember how many times they'd squared off in the ring, but Lou had crossed the Pacific to attend his retirement ceremony and push his wheelchair for him. Twelve bells. He remembered the twelve-bell salute that had marked his retirement. The moment when the ups and downs of his career as a pro-wrestler had come to an end. No matter how hard he tried, he couldn't remember much of what had happened inside the ring, not even the roar of the crowds. What he did remember vividly though was having the breath squeezed out of him by the weight of his opponent and squirming so hard to escape the other man's grasp and get his breath back that he felt like his ears were being torn from the sides of his head. Each time his airway reopened, he made the same vow: to never step back into the ring again.

People often asked him if it was true that wrestling was all fake. He answered by showing them his cauliflower ears.

'It's real up until one of you is at the brink of death, then we fake it. You think faking it does this to your ears?'

The photographer paused in front of a recent photo of the wrestler with a medal hanging from his neck.

'You can skip that one,' the wrestler said.

The photographer started, then nodded and bowed in greeting.

'I didn't realise you were standing there. It's a pleasure to meet you.'

They shook hands.

The photographer had mailed him three or four batches of photos. Pics of the newly built memorial outside of his house to commemorate his career, and of the modest events held in his home town that he'd been unable to attend. Each photo had been accompanied by a note explaining the related occasion in detail. For some reason, he had assumed from these pictures that the photographer was much older. But in person, he looked barely over forty. He had a buck-toothed smile and a baby face. Maybe it was the photographer's apparent lack of pretension, but he didn't feel like he was meeting a stranger.

15

'Are these all of them?' the photographer asked, turning to take in the rest of the living room.

'Goodness, no,' the nurse answered for him, walking in with a glass of orange juice on a tray. 'There are more in that small room over there, and photos out in the shed that we haven't even unboxed yet. It'll take you forever to make copies of all –'

'I told you not to bother with the recent ones,' the wrestler interjected. 'Just the ones from my wrestling days.'

The plan was to get copies of all the mounted photos and send them to Japan. Most of the photos from his glory days had been taken in Japan and almost all of the material related to his career was stored in gyms and by acquaintances there. Photos were the only thing he could trust now. They were much more accurate than his memories. He'd hoped to use the photos to piece together what he had lost, but he discovered he couldn't remember exactly where, when, with whom, and just how they had been taken. Eventually, someone else would do the work of captioning each with well thought-out explanations, but he wished he could do that for himself in the moment.

'They agreed to help if I send them the film,' the photographer said.

'Did you talk to Kamei-san?'

'Not yet, but the gym said they would.'

'He took a lot of the photos back when he was working at a newspaper. He sent over everything he had, but there might be more. He was so meticulous. Anyway, you've got your work cut out for you.'

The photographer smiled modestly. 'I'll take more photos after the wedding.'

The nurse headed into the bedroom carrying his suit. The wrestler followed her.

16

It was hotter outside than he'd expected. The sunlight bouncing off the marble monuments outside the gate felt like it could sear the surroundings out of existence. While the photographer turned the car around, the wrestler kept his eyes trained on the small memorial garden that had been built in his honour. Three stone tablets stood side by side. The tablet to the left was topped with a bronze statue of a dog, while the tablet to the right was engraved with his certificate of merit. The tablet in the middle was blank. It would hold his bust after he had passed away.

He didn't care what the people of his home town did, and they never bothered discussing any of it with him first. When the garden was first built, he was lying in the hospital with no idea what would become of him. But seeing how people visited him now, bearing their little gift bottles of juice and Vegemil, as if to witness his last will and testament regardless of whether his condition was getting better or worse, made it seem only natural that they would have built the garden in anticipation of his death.

It had shocked him to see photos of the place. The blank marble tablet, which looked like it was awaiting a coffin, was bad enough, but what really shook him was the statue of the dog. Why a dog? he'd wondered, as he read the caption below the photo, most of which quoted the epitaph carved into the tablet, but which ended with:

I pray that we think of the sad tears of my friends – no, everyone's friends – the Jindo dogs, gone to an untimely death,

17

and ensure that not a single dog, nor even a single blade of
grass on this earth, is ever again sacrificed to foreign powers.
I beg forgiveness now for our mistakes and dedicate this small
memorial to them.

He remembered an interview he'd given for some newspaper
a very long time ago. He'd shared memories of a dog, but he
wasn't sure if it had been a Jindo dog. He was even less sure
that it had been the Japanese who'd slaughtered the dogs,
using their skins for military supplies and their meat for military
rations. After receiving the photos, he'd been plagued by a vague
sense of foreboding that he would never go home again. It may
have been a form of remorse. He didn't understand why he felt
that way, considering how unclear his memories were. He had
never doubted his life as a wrestler, had always believed that
each era has its own dreams.

The ring was a re-enactment of life. The only time that
existed within the ring were the taut minutes of a wrestling
match. There was friend, there was foe. An impoverished boy
entered the ring in search of fame and fortune, while the feeble
masses sought to superimpose themselves onto the strong-
man standing at the battle's end. The truly clever ones might
convince themselves that their lives were not so unfortunate
after all. Just imagine the dreams of those poor, ragged children
of the motherland who watched as their hero was tossed this
way and that, by Japanese fighters, by Western fighters, only to
emerge victorious! Of course, that dream had not lasted long.
When the General died, professional wrestling died with him. And
for better or worse, this wrestler had not died in the ring but
walked out on his own two feet and so remained ever-victorious
in his fans' memories. Though his life turned out differently than
he might have wanted, he accepted this as the fate history had

18

dished out to everyone of his generation. He wasn't so oblivious to reality. It was only natural for a public figure to live this way. But now, looking at those stone tablets, he couldn't shake the chill creeping over his heart.

He didn't snap out of this reverie until they were driving onto the main street of the township.

'You must really like living here,' the wrestler said. 'But then, I guess, since you're a photographer, that you see the value in things the rest of us overlook.'

'It's more that I haven't been able to leave,' the photographer said, sounding embarrassed.

'I left because I was hungry. I was much younger than you back then. If I could've made a living here, I would have stayed.'

'My father left, too, but came back.'

'What's his name?'

'Jang Keum-sik, from Yeonjeong Village.' The photographer quietly clucked his tongue. 'He's been bedridden for years.'

Jang Keum-sik. The name rang a bell. When it came to meeting people from his home town, faces were always more familiar than names. If he were to see the photographer's father in person, he would almost certainly know him.

They passed a National Agricultural Co-operative Federation truck loaded high with onions. The piles of red mesh bags had been catching his eye everywhere he turned. The road looked nothing like it had back in the 1950s, when he'd boarded a smuggling ship and run from home, but the smell of dereliction had somehow grown thicker. It might have been coming from the seedy motels tucked between the low slab buildings, or the faded teahouse signs hanging from every third or fourth house.

'Sir.' This time, the photographer was the first to speak. He looked sheepish. 'I heard a story growing up about how you first learned that you had a knack for headbutting. I was wondering if it was true?'

'...'

'You used to chop firewood in the mountains with your father, right?'

'Yes, all the time,' the wrestler said, gazing out at the distant mountains. 'We'd go all the way up there, to Geumjangdae, and beyond. There was nowhere we didn't go. We made a living off of chopping firewood.'

'Really? So that part of the legend is true.'

The photographer looked elated, as if an old mystery had been solved. The wrestler waited, curious.

'They said that, one day, you swung the axe and the blade flew off the handle and smacked you in the forehead, but it didn't even leave a scratch. Was that true?'

'That's what they said about me?' The wrestler chuckled.

'We all grew up hearing these stories.'

Judging from the photographer's face, he still earnestly believed these tales, despite being a grown man. The wrestler didn't often contradict the stories people told about him and this was no exception. But a feeling of impotence swept over him. He felt suddenly exhausted.

Back when he'd first started wrestling, his trainer had toughened his forehead with ashtrays and golf clubs. Despite having the strength and flexibility to sweep every match, he didn't really have a natural pro-wrestler build. But his trainer's pet theory was that, to become a pro, all you really needed was the personality of an entertainer. That could mean having the right look, the right costume, or deploying any number of dirty tricks, but his trainer wanted him to use his head – literally. And he'd make the right call. What a stroke of genius, to have figured out that, rather than swinging a bicycle chain, two-by-four, or iron rod at your opponent, subduing them with a simple head-butt would be so satisfying! His trainer used to crow that the headbutt was a fitting move for 'gooks like us'.

But his head had ached all the time, his eyes spun, and he felt constantly on the verge of throwing up, and so he became judicious about how he put his skill to use. When his opponent fouled him or defeat was imminent and the audience pumped their fists and clamoured impatiently, that's when he would pull out his signature move and turn the tide in his favor. He knew, each time he stepped into the ring, exactly what his cheering fans were hoping for and he always delivered. As the crowds rose in unison and began to pump their fists still more furiously into the air, he would go into a stupor and unleash a volley of head-butts to knock his opponent out. What kept him going in that moment was sheer willpower, the refusal to fall. The cheering of the crowd would have long since faded from his ears, leaving behind only the thought that the clanging of the bell would allow him to finally step out of the ring and collapse, his head aching as badly as his opponent's. The only difference between him and them was that he always knew what pain was coming. He'd fought over three thousand matches this way.

As soon as they reached the wedding hall, he realised at once how foolish the decision to make an appearance had been. He hadn't even wanted to come. A gray-haired man called out to him and clasped his hand. He could not for the life of him place the man's face.

'I should have come as soon as I heard the news, but I haven't been in great shape myself either.'

Tears brimmed in the man's eyes and threatened to spill over. A young woman was at his side, a daughter, perhaps, or daughter-in-law, helping him to walk. His hand trembled as he stroked the wrestler's hands over and over, but as a symptom of illness rather than excitement.

"How could this happen? How could this happen to one of our great athletes?"

He had no choice but to grasp the man's arm in return. It changed nothing. He assumed that he and this man must have grown up together, but he still had no clue who he was. His desire and need to remember grew, while his memory remained stubbornly rooted. Mercifully, the people around them were already beginning to move, so they could no longer stand there together and he followed the photographer up to the second floor in order to avoid being accosted further. He kept a bashful look on his face as he nudged his way through the people coming to greet him. *He doesn't look as bad as I'd thought*, he heard them whisper. *Wow, he's so old now*. He felt progressively more flustered, even to the point of dizziness, and nearly tripped over his own feet more than once.

By the time he managed to find his place and sit down, his back was damp. Everyone's eyes were fixed on him. He kept telling himself that he shouldn't have come to the wedding, that he was overdoing it. He couldn't help worrying that his presence was more of a blight than a blessing. He took a deep breath and looked around. The man who'd spoken to him outside was being escorted to a seat on the bride's side. From that distance, he could tell the man had had a stroke. Who was he? He tried again to remember.

22

'You came!'

He tensed on reflex and turned to look at who was sitting next to him. A familiar face this time. Kim Ga, a man two years his younger and from the neighbouring village. From an early age, they'd been as close as brothers, and had pursued wrestling careers together. They were like siblings of the ring. After going pro and visiting his home country, Ga was the only person from his home town with whom he'd stayed in contact. He knew also that the memorial park in front of his birthplace had been Ga's doing.

'I've been up to my neck in onions. I pass by your house a dozen times a day but still haven't had a chance to pop in for a visit.'

'I meant to call you as well.'

'My nephew's the one getting married. We would've picked you up at the station, but we didn't want to bother you.'

'That's okay, it all worked out.'

'How's your health? That nurse of yours seems nice.'

'Ah, so you're the old Mun Ik-jeom of onions that she was talking about.'

'She told you that? I was just joking. That woman is something else – acts like some kind of princess. Same as the rest of those city slickers who think rice grows on trees. But she's friendly. I like that.'

Ga laughed out loud. His chattiness was putting the wrestler at ease.

'But is it true that you're the Mun Ik-jeom of this place?' he asked.

'Me? People are going to think I'm sleeping with her or something. But yes, back in 1972, when I first became village foreman, I tried to set an example by planting onions myself.'

'There weren't any before that?'

23

'Not the early maturing variety. Before that, we only had the kind that you plant in vegetable gardens in June. I don't know why no one has engraved a monument to me yet.'

'So there *were* onions before,' the wrestler muttered. He felt the back of his head tingle and turned to see the gray-haired gentleman smiling at him with the half of his mouth that hadn't been paralysed.

'Do you know who that guy is? I can't seem to place him.'

'Nope. Never seen him before.'

'You don't know him either?' He sat up straighter. 'He's a stranger?'

Ga cocked an eyebrow and said, 'I have no idea. Maybe he came from the other island, where my nephew's wife is from.' He trailed off on the last words, half-talking to himself.

'He acts like he knows me...'

'Well, hey, who *doesn't* know you?'

The wrestler let out a long sigh and sank back in his chair. But then he couldn't help but chuckle. At least this time there was nothing wrong with his memory. Nothing at all! He turned to look at the gray-haired man again. This time straight in the face. As if to say, *I don't know you. And you don't know me either, do you?* It had an immediate effect. The stiff smile on the man's face crumpled, then turned sad, and finally he lowered his head.

Throughout the wedding ceremony, the wrestler stole glances at the faces of the other guests. As he counted how many were advanced in age, he let out a sigh of relief. There were a lot of faces he remembered. An elderly man sat with his eyes shut at the end of the row next to his. His flat pug nose conjured the name Yeongbok. Then he immediately pictured a little boy with a lisp, a fistful of mushy cow dung in each hand, calling out, 'Pith, thit, pith, thit'. The rush of recollection brought tears to his eyes.

24

He took his time looking around at the other guests, soaking it all in. It was like a fun game. The photographer snapped shot after shot of the bride and groom. Had he said his father's name was Jang Keum-sik? He repeated the name to himself. It still didn't sound familiar. He turned to look at the seats in the back. Country women sat in rows. He accidentally locked eyes with one dressed in a lovely hanbok and reeled back in shock. After a moment, he turned to steal another sly glance. The woman was staring off into space. His heart pounded and he tried to shake a memory from his head. Something he didn't wish to recall shoved its way to the front of his mind.

He would have been around twenty years old, back when his libido was out of control both day and night. He'd spent five days with a girl inside a hollow hayrick made from rice straw in a terraced paddy in a slash-and-burn farm village out past Keumjangdae peak. They were like coiled snakes, their desire for each other unquenchable. The only thing they ate were two rice cake sticks the girl had brought with her. By the end of the fifth day, he had a metallic smell in his nose, but still their lust would not abate. He wanted to spend the rest of his life inside that hayrick. If the girl's shaman mother hadn't set fire to it, they might've stayed inside for ever, until they were both dried up and shriveled like dead silkworms. Not long after, he left on a smuggling ship and never saw her again. Life was full of regret and youth was a time of shame.

Had he been in love with her? He shut his eyes tight. Maybe he was imagining things. Maybe his brain was playing tricks on him as it blackened and stiffened... He shook his head.

The ceremony must have ended because everyone grew noisy again.

'Brother, you don't look good,' Ga said.

'I'd better get back home to rest.'

'How about just one photo together, before you go? Is that okay?'

He nodded. He didn't want Ga to lose face on his account. He followed him to the raised platform at the front of the hall. Ga forced him to stand next to the groom, while the other guests hung back in the aisle, hesitant to join in. The wrestler felt exposed – he may as well have been standing there in front of everyone naked. He rubbed his face with one hand.

'I want a photo with him.'

One of the elderly women rushed forward, which triggered the rest to come and join. Now so many people crowded the platform that the photographer had to take five steps back to fit them all into the frame.

'Okay, eyes wide open, everyone. One... two...'

The flash went off on three and the wrestler felt his legs buckle. Someone caught him from behind. He gestured at them to let him sit, before dropping onto his butt. He raised his knees in order to try and hide his face behind them. Who was that person in the white hanbok? What was that image that had flashed so sharply before his eyes?

His vision wavered.

He heard someone say, 'Okay everyone, let's all head into the banquet room now. No, don't worry. He'll be fine.'

He lifted his head to look at the photographer.

'You...'

But that was all he could get out. He couldn't remember what it was that he had meant to say.

Just off from the main hall was an office with a sofa where he could rest. Ga was jittery. The wrestler tried to reassure him.

'I'll be fine in a minute. I'm already feeling much better.'

'I shouldn't have pushed you to take a photo.'

He waved his hand at that as if to brush the remark away. A glass of water appeared. He sat up to quench his parched mouth.

'Let me ask you something. Who is Jang Keum-sik?'

'Do you mean Uncle Jeong-hui?'

'Uncle Jeong-hui?'

'The person who runs the night school, Uncle Jeong-hui. His real name is Jang Keum-sik. The guy out there taking photos is his son.'

'Night school? So he never left…'

He lay back down on the sofa. Now he understood the vision that had flashed before him a moment before. He'd remembered taking a group photo in front of the night school with a number of other young islanders and Uncle Jeong-hui, their teacher. It was from before the war.

'None of us thought we'd ever see him again,' Ga said. 'But he returned about ten years after finishing his prison sentence. He married late and had a baby, so of course he had to stick around to see the baby grow up.'

'I heard he can't walk.'

'Walking's not the only thing. He's pretty much a breathing corpse at this point. It was his own damn temper that did him in. About ten years ago, the regional business association decided to write down the history of the township, but they couldn't find anyone who was up to the task. They finally settled on Uncle Jeong-hui. I was sure he would turn them down. But to my surprise, he agreed. For five years, that's all he worked on. He must've filled at least fifty notebooks. But they weren't happy with it. He'd written down in detail all of the political squabbling that had taken place, between the left and the right. The association asked him to take those parts out. They pleaded with him

27

to fix it, but he refused. Since then, the work has been rotting away in storage at the township office. It must have knocked the last wind out of his sails because soon after that he collapsed and his health began to deteriorate.'

'Did he write about me as well?'

'Given how much of his own life he'd considered worth noting, do you think he'd leave yours out? In fact, it was the parts about you that most concerned those who were opposed to the whole thing.'

'What did it say?'

'Well...'

Ga took a moment to clear his throat.

'Do you think I'm a traitor for running away?'

'Oh, come on, that's all in the past. Why dredge that up? Things that happened back then shouldn't continue to define us.'

'I left because I was hungry!'

The words came out louder than he'd expected. Ga took it in stride. A long silence followed. It was clear to him now. What was the point of chasing after memories, when he'd had everything so twisted up all along? He'd spent too long inside the ring. It couldn't end like this. Why hadn't the General aimed a rifle at his head instead? Why didn't the islanders carve the whole truth into those stones?

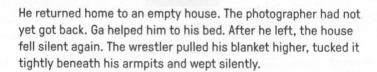

He returned home to an empty house. The photographer had not yet got back. Ga helped him to his bed. After he left, the house fell silent again. The wrestler pulled his blanket higher, tucked it tightly beneath his armpits and wept silently.

It grew noisy outside and he heard a group of people shuffle into the living room. He heard the nurse welcome them in.

'He's still at the wedding, so take your time looking around.'

'We'd been talking about stopping by some time.'

The living room filled with the sound of women's voices.

'Oh my! Look at all these photos of him!'

'I don't know how he can bear to die and leave this all behind.'

'You're telling me. If I were him, I would never let go.'

The wrestler bit down harder on the edge of his blanket.

Yeoyu is a series of chapbooks showcasing the work of some of the most exciting writers working in Korean today, published by Strangers Press, part of the UEA Publishing Project.

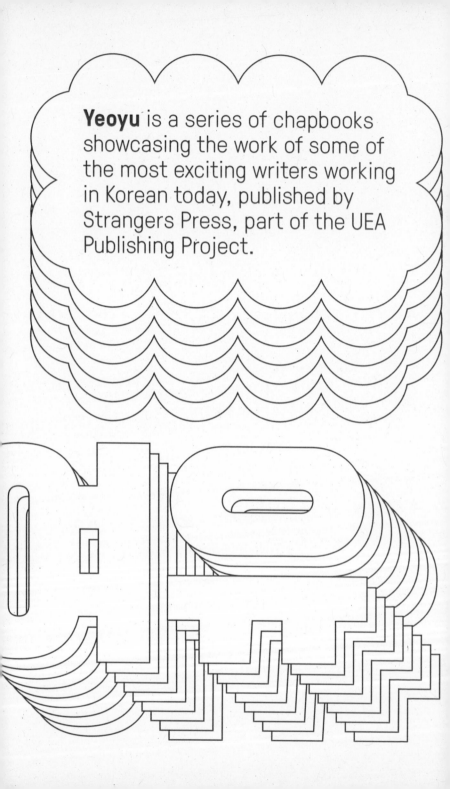

Yeoyu is a unique collaboration between an international group of independent creative practitioners, with University of East Anglia, Norwich University of the Arts, and the National Centre for Writing, made possible by LTI Korea.

LTI Korea

University of East Anglia

NORWICH
UNIVERSITY
OF THE ARTS